GET SET FOR KINDERGARTEN!

How Many? How Much?

BASED ON TIMOTHY GOES TO SCHOOL AND OTHER STORIES BY

ROSEMARY WELLS

ILLUSTRATED BY MICHAEL KOELSCH

PUFFIN BOOKS

Mrs. Jenkins's Class,

Hilltop School

DORIS

NORA

CLAUDE

FRANK

FRANK

TIMOTHY and his classmates are practicing counting. "Let's all count to ten together," says Mrs. Jenkins. "I'll point to each number as you say it. Ready. Set. Go!"

Say the numbers along with the class. Point to each number as you say it. Now look at the picture and point to the numbers that tell . . .

- **how many teachers you see.**
- **how many students you see.**
- **how many drawings you see on the wall.**

The Next Step

Look around *your* house or classroom. What can you count? Here are some ideas: windows, chairs, and people.

6 7 8 9 10

At play time, Yoko and Nora paint pictures. Timothy and Charles build a castle out of blocks. Fritz looks at books about famous inventors. When it's time to clean up, Mrs. Jenkins says, "Please put everything away and get ready for story time." The classroom is a mess! Can you help Timothy and his friends put everything away? Look at the pictures below. Each object in the top row belongs in a place pictured in the bottom row. Where does each object in the top row belong?

The Next Step

Ask an adult to help you cut three circles, three triangles, and three squares out of paper. Color one of each shape red, one of each shape blue, and one of each shape green. Now make three piles—one for the red shapes, one for the blue shapes, and one for the green shapes. Mix all of the shapes together again. Now make three different piles—one for the circles, one for the triangles, and one for the squares.

Yoko's mother is making a special sushi dinner. She says Yoko can invite Timothy.

"I'll call and ask him to come over," Yoko says.

Timothy's phone number is 555-8416. Can you help Yoko call Timothy? Using the big phone on the right, dial Timothy's phone number. Now dial your own phone number. Do you know what numbers to dial in case of an emergency?

The Next Step

Next time someone in your house needs to make a phone call, ask if you can help dial the number. If you are calling a friend, try to dial the number yourself.

Today Timothy and his classmates are going to measure things in their classroom.

"Nora, would you pass out the rulers?" asks Mrs. Jenkins.

"Yes, yes, yes!" says Nora. She gives a ruler to everyone in the class.

"Wait a minute," says Doris. "Something is wrong with my ruler!"

Look at Doris's ruler at the top of the page. Can you tell what is missing?

The Next Step

Fritz is measuring his pencil. How many inches long is it?

Look at the calendar of Timothy's week. How many days are in a week? Can you name the days of the week? On what day is Timothy going to Yoko's violin recital? On what day is he playing with Fritz? On what day is he going shopping with his mother?

The Next Step

Look at a calendar at home or at school. What day of the week is today? What day of the week is tomorrow? What day of the week was yesterday?

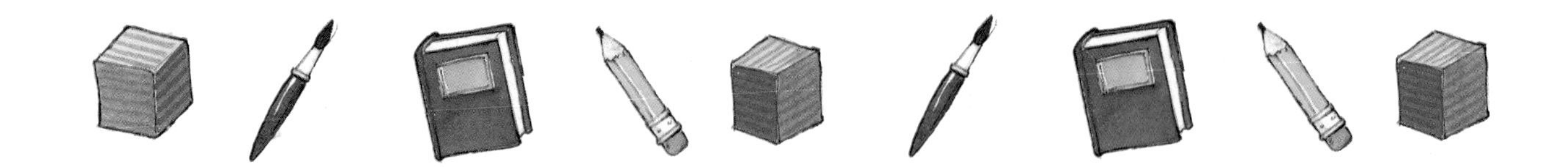

"Let's use our feet to measure distance," says Mrs. Jenkins. Nora walks from her seat to the Learning Tree, placing one foot in front of the other. Count Nora's footprints and say how many steps she took. Then Timothy walks from his seat to the Learning Tree. Count Timothy's footprints and say how many steps he took. Who sits closer to the Learning Tree—Timothy or Nora? Who sits farther away from the Learning Tree—Timothy or Nora?

The Next Step

Use your feet to measure things. In your bedroom, how many steps is your bed from the door? In your kitchen, how many steps is the table from the refrigerator? In your bathroom, how many steps is the sink from the bathtub?

9-2
8+4
8+1
7-5
4-2
1+9
2+5
3+3
5-1
4+6
6+2
2+1
6+2
7+4
4+1
7-1
4-1
3+2
1+6
2+5
7+2
1+3
6+4
3+6
3+3

"Time for a snack," says Mrs. Jenkins.
"Yay, I have an oatmeal raisin cookie," says Timothy.
"I have a banana," says Nora. "I hate bananas. I asked for candy."
"Let's share," says Timothy. "I'll give you half my cookie if you give me half your banana."
Which picture shows Nora's banana broken in half?

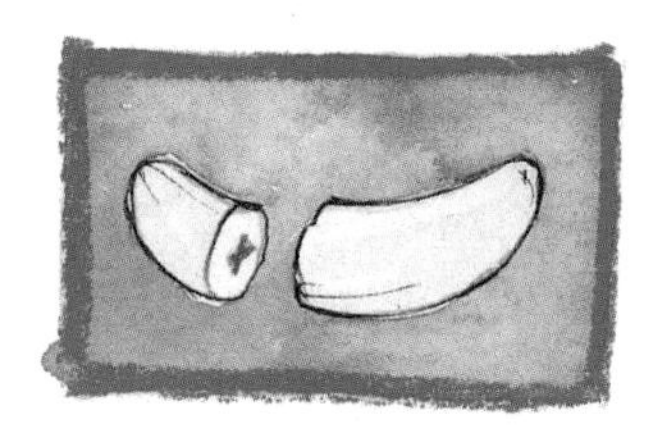

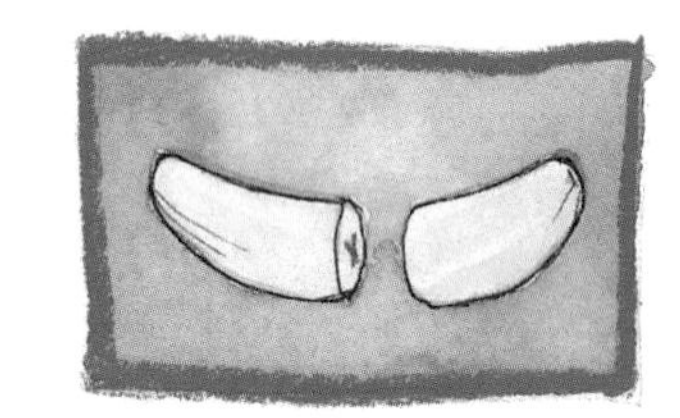

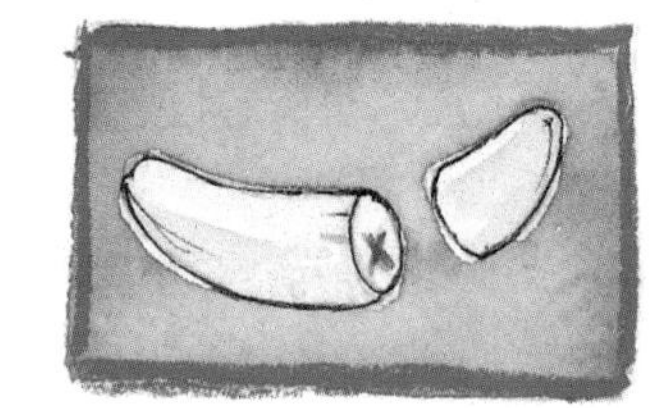

The Next Step

Ask an adult to help you cut three large shapes from a piece of paper—a square, a circle, and a rectangle. Now ask an adult to help you cut each shape in half. Is each half of each shape the same size? It should be.

Today is the school bake sale. Everyone brought in money to buy something. Timothy has seven pennies. Yoko has two pennies. Charles has five pennies. What can they each buy?

The Next Step

Play store with real money. Get some pennies and a few things to "sell"— toys, pencils, books, or whatever you like. Make price tags for the things in your store. Everything can cost ten cents or less. Use your pennies to buy things from the store.

Timothy and Yoko are building block towers. Whose tower is taller? Whose is shorter? How many blocks are in Timothy's tower? How many blocks are in Yoko's tower? Whose tower has more blocks? Whose tower has fewer blocks?

The Next Step

If Yoko adds one more block, how many blocks will be in her tower? If Timothy takes off one block, how many blocks will be in his tower?

It's art time, and Timothy's class is going to paint pictures. Mrs. Jenkins asks Doris to pass out the paintbrushes.

Doris goes to the art supplies area. There are only a few paintbrushes in the jar, and there are ten students in the class. Will there be enough to give one paintbrush to every child?

The Next Step

How many children are there in your family? How many adults are there in your family? Are there more adults than children in your family, or fewer?

Timothy and Yoko are making a design with different shapes. Name the shapes in their pattern. What shape comes next?

Fritz and Claude are making a design, too. What shape will they need to finish their pattern?

The Next Step

Make your own puzzle. Cut out a large picture from a magazine and glue it to a thick piece of paper. Ask an adult to help you cut the picture into pieces of different shapes and sizes. See if you can put your picture back together.

"Let's practice counting using number cards" says Mrs. Jenkins. "Who can help me carry the cards to the table?"

Timothy raises his hand.

"Thank you, Timothy," says Mrs. Jenkins. She hands Timothy the stack of number cards. On his way to the table, he trips and drops all of the cards.

"That's okay," says Mrs. Jenkins. "We will help you put them back in order."

Can you help, too? Look at the mixed-up number cards and say what order they should go in.

The Next Step

Cut out ten paper squares and label them 1 to 10. Shuffle the cards, then try to put them in order from 10 to 1.

Claude is building a road using blocks. He is almost done—he needs just one more block to finish the road. Can you tell which shape block he will need?

The Next Step

Use blocks to build your own model—a house, a bridge, a castle, or whatever you'd like. Do you need different-size blocks for different parts of your model? Why?

The school day is almost over.

"Tomorrow is FIVE DAY," says Mrs. Jenkins. "All day long we're going to talk about the number five. Everyone should bring in five of something for show-and-tell."

"I'm going to bring in five origami birds," says Yoko.

"I'm going to bring in five lollipops," says Nora.

"I'm going to bring in five marbles from my marble collection," says Timothy.

If you were in Timothy's class, what would you bring to school for FIVE DAY?

The Next Step

Look around the room you are in. Do you see five of anything? Try to make collections of five—five rocks, five leaves, five buttons, or whatever you'd like!

Letter to Parents and Educators

The early years are a dynamic and exciting time in a child's life, a time in which children acquire language, explore their environment, and begin to make sense of the world around them. In the preschool and kindergarten years, parents and teachers have the joy of nurturing and promoting this continued learning and development. The books in the *Get Set for Kindergarten!* series were created to help in this wonderful adventure.

The activities in this book are designed to be developmentally appropriate and geared toward the interests, needs, and abilities of prekindergarten and kindergarten children. After each activity, a suggestion is made for "The Next Step," an extension of the skill being practiced. Some children may be ready to take the next step; others may need more time.

During the preschool years, children begin to develop mathematical awareness. They acquire simple mathematical concepts, including counting, time, and distance, that form the basis for learning to add, subtract, multiply, and divide. *How Many? How Much?* aims to stimulate and promote this learning.

Throughout the early years, children need to be surrounded by language and learning and love. Those who nurture and educate young children give them a gift of immeasurable value that will sustain them throughout their lives.

John F. Savage, Ed.D.
Educational Consultant